BOO!

BOO!

A HALLOWEEN STORY

BY JACQUE HALL

ILLUSTRATED BY JENNIFER OERTEL

ABOOKS

Alive Book Publishing

Additional copies may be ordered from the publisher for educational, business,
promotional or premium use. For information, contact ALIVE Book Publishing at:
alivebookpublishing.com, or call (925) 837-7303.

Book Design by Jennifer Oertel
Book Layout by Alex Johnson

ISBN 13
978-1-63132-054-5

ISBN 10
1-63132-054-8

Library of Congress Control Number: 2018949495

Library of Congress Cataloging-in-Publication Data is available upon request.

First Edition

Published in the United States of America by ALIVE Book Publishing
and ALIVE Publishing Group, imprints of Advanced Publishing LLC
3200 A Danville Blvd., Suite 204, Alamo, California 94507
alivebookpublishing.com

10 9 8 7 6 5 4 3 2 1

TO BELOVED KEVIN-

YOUR CHILDHOOD TRICKS WERE ALWAYS A TREAT

CANDLES
FLICKERING

JACK
O' LANTERNS GLOWING

MONSTERS
CLOMPING

SKELETONS HURRYING

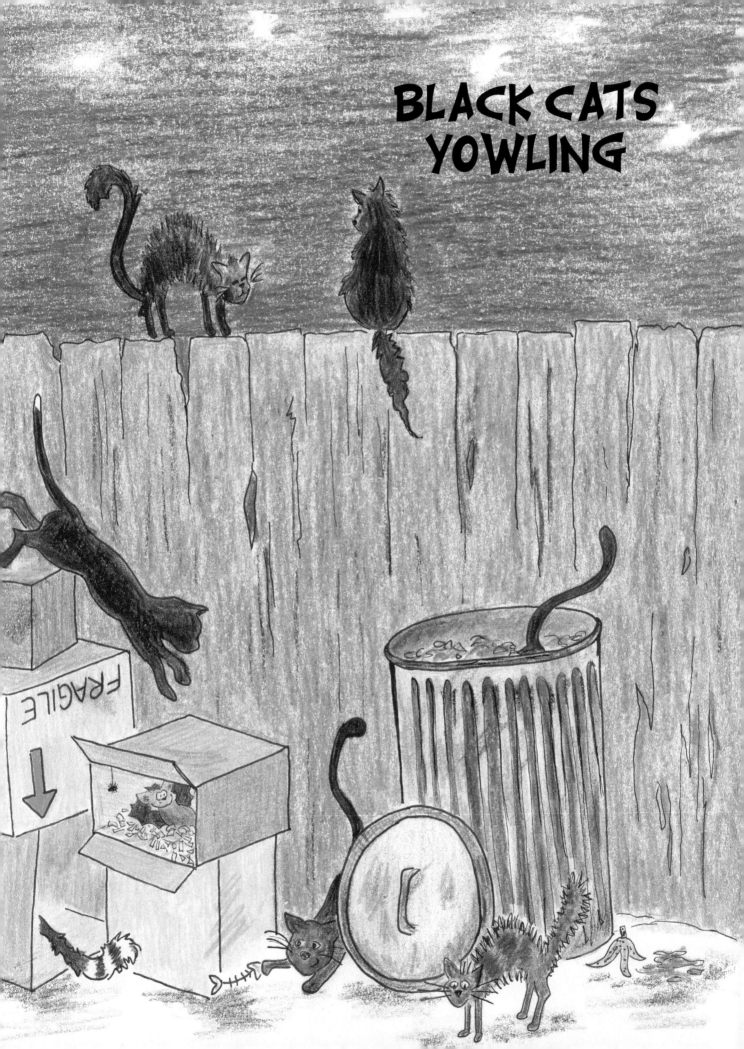

CHILDREN LAUGHING...

"TRICK OR TREAT!"

PSST...

HEY KIDS, CAN YOU FIND ONE OF OUR "BATTY" LITTLE FRIENDS ON EVERY PAGE?

SEE IF YOU CAN!

ALSO BY JACQUE HALL:

What Does the Rabbit Say?

Children's picture book for 2-6 years old.

Published by Random House/Doubleday

The Four from California

Humorous travel memoir from a trip to England.

Available at Xlibris.com

Life as an Anecdote

Collection from Jacque's newspaper column, both funny and touching.

Available at Lulu.com

Tommy Turns Detective

A young sleuth sets out to solve a ghost mystery; for middle readers.

Available at Lulu.com

Tell Me a Story, Nona

Rhymes, wordplay, and stories for young children.

Available at Lulu.com

The ABC's of Carrots and Peas

Rhyming picture book about grocery shopping.

Available from Alive Book Publishing

ABOOKS

ALIVE Book Publishing and ALIVE Publishing Group
are imprints of Advanced Publishing LLC,
3200 A Danville Blvd., Suite 204, Alamo, California 94507

Telephone: 925.837.7303 Fax: 925.837.6951
www.alivebookpublishing.com